HURRY!

by **Jessie Haas** • pictures by **Jos. A. Smith**

Greenwillow Books
An Imprint of HarperCollins*Publishers*

THANKS TO JAY BAILEY OF FAIR WINDS FARM
—J. H. AND J. A. S.

Watercolor paints, colored pencils, and watercolor pencils were used for
the full-color art. The text type is Meridien. Hurry! Text copyright © 2000
by Jessie Haas. Illustrations copyright © 2000 by Jos. A. Smith.
Printed in Hong Kong by South China Printing Company (1988) Ltd.

Library of Congress Cataloging-in-Publication Data

Haas, Jessie.
Hurry! / by Jessie Haas ; pictures by Jos. A. Smith.
    p.   cm.
"Greenwillow Books."
Summary: A young girl helps her grandparents get
the hay in before a rainstorm ruins the crop.
ISBN 0-688-16889-2.   [1. Hay—Harvesting—Fiction.
2. Grandparents—Fiction.]   I. Smith, Jos. A.
(Joseph Anthony), (date) ill.   II. Title.
PZ7.H1129Hat   2000   [E]—dc21   99-30706   CIP

1 2 3 4 5 6 7 8 9 10 First Edition

Hurry! Hurry! whispers the
breeze. It lifts the silver poplar
leaves. Rain coming!
Hurryuphurryuphurryup the
haytedder clacks, as Nora
drives it around the field.
The forks of the tedder kick
like dancing legs. They kick
the grass high in the air and
turn it over so the sun can dry
the underside.
When all the grass is dry
and sweet smelling, it will
be hay.

"Hurry up and wait," says Gramp.
"We can't make the hay dry faster.
The sun has to do that."
But he worries, and so does Nora.
Hay can't get rained on, or it
spoils. Bonnie and Stella and the
cows need hay to eat this winter.
"Nothing's more important on
this farm than hay," Gramp says.

He goes out to check the hay, and then he checks again. The sky turns milky white. Then it's gray, and then it's grayer. The sun feels weak, but the wind feels strong. Gramp says, "Nora, your legs are young. Go out and see if it's dry."

Nora picks up a handful
of hay. It's silvery green.
It smells as sweet as
flowers. She crinkles
it in her hand. It makes
a rustling, papery,
hurry-up sound.
"IT'S READY!"

Gramp drives the rake around the field. The horses walk so fast they almost trot. The rake whirs softly, combing the hay into long windrows under the dark sky.

Hurry now! Back to the barn.
Unhitch the rake, hitch onto
the wagon, hitch the wagon
to the hayloader. Here comes
Gram with the pitchforks.
"Let's go!"

Nora drives along the windrow, Bonnie's feet on one side, Stella's on the other. The hayloader swooshes up the hay and pours it onto the wagon. Gram and Gramp move it out to the corners with their pitchforks. They tread on it with their feet, they pack it tight, they pile on more.

Up and up the load rises, and
Nora rises with it. The load
of hay is as big as the moon.
It curves up so close to the
clouds, Nora could reach up
and touch them. Bonnie and
Stella look small and far
away—
"Oh!" says Nora. The big moon
tips. Will the hay slide off?
"Whoa!"
"Good job, Nora. That's all
we can fit," Gramp says. He
climbs down and unhitches
the hayloader.

Nora looks down on the little windrows.
That's good hay too. She wishes she could
cover it all. Gramp takes the reins and speaks
to the horses. They walk slowly. Every bump
and dip in the ground makes the load
tremble. It's a long way to the barn.
A raindrop lands on Nora's arm.
"We'll make it," Gram says.
Another raindrop hits Nora's
nose, and then there are more.
She spreads herself over the hay.
But she covers only a little of the
giant hay-moon. Fat raindrops
splat on her back.

The horses' hooves thud on
the barn floor, and the wagon
wheels rumble. The dark roof
shuts out the sky.
The barn smells so sweet.
All of summer is inside here.
The rain patters, then it
splashes, then it drums.
It makes a silver curtain
between the barn and the
wide, green world.
"Oh, the poor hay!" Nora says.
"I wish we'd gotten it all."
"We got a lot," says Gram.
Gramp gives the horses an
armful of hay.

Then he and
Gram and Nora
sit on the wagon
and watch the
rain come down.